BY Jane Breskin Zalben

ILLUSTRATED BY
Emilie Chollat

Hey, Mama Goose

HOME
SWEET
HOME

MAMA Goose
REAL
ESTATE

Dutton Children's Books · NEW YORK

Text copyright © 2005 by Jane Breskin Zalben
Illustrations copyright © 2005 by Emilie Chollat

CIP Data is available.

Published in the United States by Dutton Children's Books,
a division of Penguin Young Readers Group
345 Hudson Street, New York, New York 10014
www.penguin.com

Designed by Irene Vandervoort
Manufactured in China
First Edition
ISBN 0-525-47097-2

10 9 8 7 6 5 4 3 2 1

To my lovable threesome (SZ, AZ, & JZ)—wherever you are is "home."
And to Stephanie Owens Lurie—for giving me another kind of home.
J.B.Z.

To my friend Sophie
E.C.

There was an old woman who lived in a shoe.
She cried, "Hey, Mama Goose, what should I do?
My family is growing and with it my fears
That a shoe isn't roomy enough for my dears."

Mama Goose said, "Old Woman, you need a new place.
I know just the right cottage with plenty of space.
Pack up your bags and lace your shoe tight
And move everyone to the home of Snow White."

"Snow White and the dwarfs left to live with a maid
Who is known far and wide for her long yellow braid.

Since the dwarfs are away, there are now seven beds
With seven plump pillows for seven small heads."

Rapunzel invited Snow White to her castle,
Complaining to her, "My hair is a hassle."

She rented a room from a gnome who had said,
"I can spin your hair into pure golden thread."

Rumpelstiltskin remarked, "I'm tired of tresses!
The time is now ripe for changing addresses."

He yearned to spin sugar, not spools of fine metal,
So he sought out the cottage of Hansel and Gretel.

"Take it!" cried Hansel, explaining their woes.
"The sweets made us too fat to fit in our clothes."
They jogged up and down, determined to shed
The pounds they had gained from the iced gingerbread.

Hansel and Gretel, hungry for greens,
Salads of parsley, lettuce, and beans,

Snacked in a garden, eating their fill,
When down tumbled Jack, followed by Jill.

Jill's knee was scraped, and Jack held his crown
As they searched high and low for a haven in town.

Mama Goose said to Jill, "I'm surely not bluffing.
This house is resistant to huffing and puffing."

The brave little pigs, with a yen for exploring,
Hiked to a palace that rumbled with snoring.

Through briars and roses, a princess awoke
To an oink and a grunt when the evil spell broke.

Sleeping Beauty opened her eyes with a start.
"Prince Charming you're not—no pig wins my heart!"

She raced to a bungalow, built by three bears,
With three bowls of porridge and also three chairs.

The family of bears had traveled away
To drum up some business for opening day
Of their soon-to-be famous hot-porridge stand
In a vacant worn shoe in Tale-telling Land.

Customers came from the farthest of places.
They chattered at tables and swung on the laces.

They savored not only the porridge so hot
But also this excellent picnicking spot.

Next door the old woman took one look at the scene
And gathered her brood, thinking, What can this mean?

From the looks on their faces, the old woman could see
That every last child was as homesick as she.
"This house is no better, and in some ways it's worse
Than the shoe that I treated like some kind of curse."

Parting the curtains, she surveyed the pack,
Then hollered to all, "It's time to GO BACK!"

With bowls washed and stacked, the bears shut down the store.
All returned to the homes they had lived in before.

They sat at their hearths and put kettles on
And couldn't recall why they ever had gone.

"Why, our shoe is enormous!" the Old Woman said
As her children lay squeezed like sardines in their beds.
She rocked in her chair and gazed at her crew
And sighed to herself, "There's no place like a shoe."